VICTORIAN
GHOST
STORIES

for
David

CHRISTMAS IN DEVON

VICTORIAN
GHOST
STORIES

Todd Gray

First published in Great Britain by The Mint Press, 2001

© Todd Gray & The Mint Press 2001

The right of Todd Gray to be identified as author of this work has been asserted by him in accordance with the Copyright, Designs & Patents Act 1988.

All rights reserved. No part of this publication may be reproduced in any form or by any means without the prior permission of the copyright holders

ISBN 1–903356–19–9

Cataloguing in Publication Data
CIP record for this title is available from the British Library

The Mint Press
18 The Mint
Exeter, Devon
England EX4 3BL

Text and cover design by Delphine Jones

Printed and bound in Great Britain
by Short Run Press Ltd, Exeter.

CONTENTS

Introduction	6
The Red Barn at Crediton TICKLER	7
Jasper Berryman's Christmas Party: A legend of old Exeter HENRY SKINNER	16
The Haunted Roadside Cottage TJN	35
The Ghosts of Grimsby Grange TJN	44
Ghost Story TICKLER	66
A Devonshire Ghost Story G. SEAGE	77
The Devil and the Money-Hunters at Afton Castle TICKLER	87

INTRODUCTION

Each story which makes up this collection was published in *The Devon Weekly Times* except 'Jasper Berryman's Christmas Party: A legend of old Exeter' by Henry Skinner which appeared in *The Exeter Flying Post* on 23 December 1893. 'Ghost Story' by Tickler was printed on 23 December 1864, 'The Red Barn at Crediton' and 'The Devil and the Money-Hunters at Afton Castle', also by Tickler, were published on December 22 1865, 'The Haunted Roadside Cottage' and 'The Ghosts of Grimsby Grange', both by 'TJN', were published on 23 December 1881 and 23 December 1880, and G. Seage's 'A Devonshire Ghost Story' on 24 December 1896.

Normally local newspapers reprinted stories from national publications but readers were given local stories at Christmas. 'Tickler' wrote regularly for *The Devon Weekly Times* and was most probably on the staff. Henry Skinner may have been the writer H. J. Skinner who published *The Lily of the Lyn and other Poems* in 1884. 'TJN' has not been identified and G. Seage does not appear to have written more extensively than this short story.

The writers drew upon the readers' interest in their local areas but most of the place names were imaginary.

The Red Barn at Crediton

TICKLER

1865

Crediton, like all other country towns, still abounds with people who relate marvellous stories of witches and haunted houses; and many a place reported to be 'troubled' by the ghosts of former owners is still pointed out by the ancients. I shall select for my present story an old barn in close proximity to the Western part of the town, the beautiful hills on the North side of which would long ago have attracted the attention of more speculative people than the Creditonians, as an earthly paradise for a number of detached villas, the occupants of which might have an unlimited view of the Dartmoor mountains on one side, and of an indescribably rich, well-wooded country on the other.

So much, however, were the Creditonians of the last generation wedded to obsolete ideas, that any one who talked of widening the old packhorse lands, which led from the town in various directions, and of opening up delightful building ground, or of lighting the town with gas, was laughed down as a dreamy enthusiast, whose plans, if carried out, would entail widespread ruin on all concerned in them, and he who talked of underground drainage was called 'a fine gentleman' with too sensitive a nose and eyes, who had forgotten that many a nonegenarian had passed all his days amidst the open drains and roadways strewed with the entrails of fish, decayed vegetables and unmentionable matter.

And the late Mr A. Wreyford, who, as 'Town Way-Warden' thoroughly drained a great part of the streets, without consulting his brother way-wardens in the country, very narrowly escaped being saddled with the whole cost of the work, as even 'advanced Radicals' among the farmers could not be brought to understand that filth and bad drainage produced a plentiful crop of ague, fever and dysentery, and entailed a perpetual and heavy charge on the ratepayers, who had to provide for the widows and children of those poor persons who were stricken down by preventable diseases.

But I am digressing from the ghost story, though we often fancy that there is a clear connection between the abominations to which I have referred and stories of ghosts, for ignorance and filth are generally the offspring of superstition.

On a hill overlooking a large waste of

ground, called, *par excellence*, Crediton Green – which, however, is the receptacle for all kinds of rubbish, but which if properly fenced out and planted might be made one of the prettiest spots in Christendom – is an old barn, very much like the Red Barn in which Corder murdered Maria Martin; this often attracts the eye of the intelligent traveller who instinctively exclaims 'what a pretty spot for a house!' And, about the end of the last century, a house really did stand there, which was owned and inhabited by a hospitable old gentleman, named Purchase, of the type of Captain Jan Cooke, though he was more intelligent and better educated than that well known civic functionary.

Mr Purchase was a great stickler for 'Church and King' and, as one of the renowned of the corporation of Crediton, he rode through the streets at the head of the dragoons who suppressed a formidable bread riot there about the year 1794, and thus obtained the lasting ill-will of an unreasoning mob. Moreover, many a suspicious democrat used, I believe, to denounce him as one of Lord Eldon's spies, and the titled aristocracy of the corporation stigmatised him as an ungrateful renegade. Sir John Chichester once exclaimed, on seeing him range himself with a band of independent yeoman in the corporation 'What! is that the man to vote for whom I came all the way from London?'

Old Purchase, however, kept a very good table – one redeeming virtue – and dearly loved a game at cards; and, in spite of his anti-Romanising principles, it was said that he would occasionally indulge in his favourite diversion on a Sunday; but, whether or not this were so, certain it was that the tale ran among the ignorant and superstitious, immediately after his death, that his house was 'troubled' on account of his Sabbath desecrating propensities.

Crowds of people used to congregate in Crediton Green, about 9 or 10 o'clock at night, to witness lights moving fitfully about, from room to room, in the uninhabited house lately occupied by him, and a respectable octogenarian, of unimpeachable veracity, who on several occasions witnessed this mysterious light, has lately given me a graphic description of it, remarking that the workmen could not have been employed in the house at such an unseasonable hour, and shaking her head in an unbelieving manner, when I suggested that some mischievous wags had obtained a surreptitious entrance to the house, in order to terrify the good people of Crediton. But whether the mysterious light was occasioned in this manner, or the heated imagination of the terrified crowd magnified the irregular movements of some Jack of the Lantern, until they saw every window in turn illuminated, I will not attempt to decide. I only know that at the present day the remains of the old house – which have been long since converted into a barn – are reported to be haunted. And only two or three years ago a poor, but honest, old woman, asserted that she saw a gentleman in a carriage, with a servant, vainly driving round the field which encloses the barn in order to find a place of exit, and that at last the carriage mysteriously vanished through the hedge.

About the year 1825 an adventurous, sturdy, broad-chested youth, who had the most undaunted resolution, was returning late at night, and quite alone, from a Christmas party, and as he always chose the shortest route he had to pass through the narrow lane adjoining the barn, at a time when the moon was completely obscured.

As he went trippingly on, no doubt thinking of the pleasures of the merry dance, which he had just left at a neighbouring farmhouse, he suddenly stumbled over something that obstructed his pathway. On regaining his feet, he prepared to give the unwelcome way-layer a warm reception; but, hearing a clangour, as of the rattling of irons, he, being of a poetic, if not romantic turn of mind, thought of some drama in which he had seen a ghost depicted in chains, and for a few moments was quite unnerved, thinking that he was beset by old Purchase's troubled spirit.

'In the name of Heaven, art thou the ghost of Purchase, or art thou not?' enquired the lad.

The ghost replied by another rattle of the chain, upon which our young hero gave his imagined adversary a desperate kick, when the loud bray of a donkey immediately informed him, that if he had not been frightened by an ass in a lion's skin, it was the clank of the chain, placed round that animal's hind legs, to prevent its roaming too far, when nightly turned out to browse on the rough grass and brambles of the hedges, that had struck more terror into his soul than a lion's roar could have done.

Jasper Berryman's Christmas Party

A Legend of Old Exeter

HENRY SKINNER
1893

Twas in the year 1793, exactly one hundred years ago this very Christmas, that the little episode we are about to relate took place. The winter of that year had set in with unusual severity. The Exe was frozen over from Head Weir to Trew's Weir, and everybody was looking forward to spending a jolly Christmas and having a bit of fun on the ice.

It was late in the afternoon of Christmas Eve, that the last of the goods and chattels of the undertaker, Jasper Berryman, were heaped into a wagon, and a pair of lean horses dragged the conveyance along for the fourth time from Trinity Lane to Mary Arches Lane, for to the latter street the undertaker was removing with all his household. Having closed his old shop, he nailed a notice to the door, to the effect that the premises were to be sold or let, and started off on foot to his new abode.

He was, not unnaturally, in somewhat depressed spirits, when turning his back finally on his old home, and approaching the little yellow house, which had so long taken his fancy (being near the cemetery). Having crossed the threshold and finding his new abode in great confusion he sighed at the recollection of his old hovel, where during eighteen years everything had been conducted with the strictest regularity, and he scolded his daughters and the maid-of-all-work for their dilatoriness and set to work to assist them himself.

Order was soon established; the grandfather's clock, the dresser with the crockery, the table and sofa, occupied the corners assigned to them in the back room; in the front room was placed the master's handiwork, which consisted of coffins of all sizes and shapes; and the cupboards were filled with mourning cloaks and torches. Over the door appeared a signboard, representing a corpulent cupid holding a reversed torch, with the inscription:

> *Here are sold*
> *and ornamented*
> *plain and covered coffins*
> *coffins are also let out*
> *on hire*
> *and old ones repaired.*

Although the signboard has long since disappeared, this old house may still be recognised by its carved brackets and overhanging windows. The girls retired to their room, and Jasper, having inspected his dwelling, sat down by the window and ordered the tea to be prepared.

The enlightened reader is aware that both Shakespeare and Sir Walter Scott represented their grave-diggers as cheerful and jocose persons, in order to arouse our imagination more forcibly by the contrast between the disposition of the worker and the character of his work. Out of regard to truth, however, we cannot follow their example, and are compelled to admit that the disposition of our undertaker fully corresponded with his mournful calling. Jasper Berryman was habitually sullen and thoughtful. His silence might occasionally be broken for the sole purpose of scolding his daughters when he chanced to find them idle, gazing out of windows at the passers-by, or asking an exhorbitant price for his goods, of those who had the misfortune (and sometimes also the good fortune) to require them.

Thus it happened that Jasper, now sipping his fourth cup of tea, was as usual sunk in melancholy reflections. He thought of the pouring rain which fell at the very outset of the retired Brigadier's funeral the previous week. Many mourning cloaks had shrunk in consequence, and many hats spoiled. He foresaw unavoidable expenditure, for his old stock of mourning attire had fallen into a pitiful condition. He hoped to charge a good round sum for the funeral of the merchant Reddaway's old wife, who had now been nearly a year at death's door. But the old woman lay dying at Lympstone, and Berryman feared lest her heirs would neglect to send for him all that distance, and would come to terms with a nearer undertaker. These meditations were unexpectedly disturbed by three freemason-like taps at the door.

'Who is there?' asked Berryman.

The door opened and a man in whom the shoemaker was recognised at a glance, walked in, and cheerfully approached.

'Pardon me, good master Berryman' said he 'pardon my intruding upon you – I was anxious to make your acquaintance. I am a boot maker, my name is Nat Treadwell, and I live across the street, and thinking you were not exactly settled, I came to ask you and your daughters with us in a friendly way.'

The invitation was accepted with good will. The undertaker asked the boot maker to sit down and take a cup of tea, and, thanks to the cordial disposition of Nathan Treadwell, their conversation soon became friendly.

'How does your trade prosper?' asked Jasper.

'Ah- he- he-!' answered Treadwell, 'so, so, I cannot complain, although my goods are of course different from yours: a live man can do without boots, but a dead man cannot do without a coffin.'

'Very true' remarked Jasper: 'however, if a live man has not got wherewith to pay for his boots, one cannot take it amiss in him if he goes barefooted, but a dead beggar has a coffin gratis.'

In this manner they conversed for some time. At last the boot maker rose and taking leave of the undertaker, renewed his invitation.

The next day at one o'clock precisely, the undertaker and his daughters passed through the wicket of the newly-bought house on their way to neighbour Treadwell. The small dwelling of the boot maker was filled with guests, who chiefly consisted of little tradesmen their wives, and their workmen, with a few others including Dan Tucker, one of the old city watchmen (there were no policemen in those days) who had, in spite of his calling, managed to secure the special goodwill of his host.

Almost everybody in Exeter knew old Dan. Jasper hastened to make his acquaintance as he would that of a man of whom he might stand in need, sooner or later, and when the guests took their seats at dinner, they sat next each other. Mr and Mrs Treadwell and their daughter Penelope, who had seen but seventeen summers, whilst dining with and entertaining their guests, assisted the cook to wait upon them. Jars of beer were fetched from the alehouse at the bottom of the street, and influenced by the good cheer, Tucker ate for four, but although Jasper did not cede to him, his daughters observed a stricter ceremony.

The conversation was becoming

louder and louder, when suddenly the host begged for a few moments' attention, and drawing the cork of a bottle of 'Old Tom' exclaimed in a loud voice 'My Friends, a Merry Christmas and the health of my good Louisa!' The bottle passed freely, and the host tenderly kissed the fresh face of his forty-year-old helpmate, while the guests drank noisily to the health of the good Louisa.

'The health of my amiable guests!' exclaimed the host opening another bottle. And his guests thanked him, and again drained their glasses. Then toast followed upon toast; the health of each guest was drunk separately; they toasted Exeter; they toasted Topsham and nearly all other Devonshire towns in general, and each one in particular; they drank to masters; they drank to foremen. Jasper drank sedulously; and was so elated, that he himself proposed some jocular toast, and even went so far as to kiss Penelope under the mistletoe.

Suddenly, one of the guests, a baker, raised his glass, and exclaimed, 'To the health of those we work for!' This proposal, like all the others, was joyously and unanimously applauded. The guests saluted each other the tailor, bowed to the boot maker, the boot maker to the tailor, the baker to both; all to the baker and so on. Dan Tucker in the midst of those mutual salutations, exclaimed, turning to his neighbour.

'What now! drink, sir, to the health of thy dead ones!' All laughed, but the undertaker considering himself affronted became sullen. Nobody noticed him; the party continued its carouse and it was midnight when all rose from the table. The guests dispersed at a late hour and most of them were elevated. The baker and the bookbinder, whose face appeared as if bound in red Morocco, led the watchman between them to his box, carrying out in this case the maxim 'one good turn deserves another'. The undertaker returned home tipsy and wrathful. 'Why, indeed', reasoned he aloud; 'why is my craft worse than any other? Is an undertaker then, brother to a hangman? What had the heathens to laugh at? Is an undertaker a Christmas harlequin? I meant to have asked them to a house-warming, to have given them a feast, but let them wait till they get it. And I shall now invite, instead, those for whom I work, my orthodox dead.'

'What sir?' said the maid, who was pulling off his boots, 'what do'ee talk about? You bain't goint to ax the dead to a housewarming shurely?'

'By - I shall ask them,' continued Jasper, 'I shall ask them at once, for tomorrow. pray come my benefactors and feast with me tomorrow evening; I shall entertain you with what God has given me; So saying the undertaker tumbled into bed, and soon began to snore.

It was still dark when Jasper was roused. The merchant Reddaway's wife had died that very night, and a special messenger had been sent on horseback with this intelligence. The undertaker gave him sixpence for a dram, dressed in haste, took a chaise and drove to Lympstone. The mutes were already stationed at the gates of the house where lay the defunct; tradesmen were going in and out like ravens at their prey. The corpse lay on a table, and relations, neighbourhood friends crowded around. Jasper went up to the merchant's nephew, a young fellow in a fashionable coat, and assured him that the coffin, cloaks, pall, and other funeral furniture would be delivered with all punctuality and without fail. The heir thanked him absently, saying that he would not bargain about the expense, but would trust implicitly to his conscience. The undertaker, as usual, swore that he would not overcharge; exchanged a significant glance with his workmen and started off to make the necessary arrangements.

The whole day was spent driving to and fro between Exeter and Lympstone; towards night, all being arranged, he settled with his driver, and returned homewards on foot. It was a moonlight night.

At the top of South Street, our friend the Watchman was shouting the hour of 'a fine and frosty morning' and on recognising the undertaker wished him good night. It was very late and the old city was as quiet as the grave.

The undertaker was approaching his house, when he suddenly fancied he saw someone ahead of him, open the wicket, pass through and disappear.

'What can this mean?' thought Jasper. 'Who is it wants me again? Can it be a thief? Do lovers perhaps visit my silly girls? It bodes evil!' And the undertaker was on the point of running for a watchman to come to his aid.

Just then some other person approached the wicket and was about to enter, but on becoming aware that Jasper was nearing hurriedly, this person stopped, and raised his cocked hat; Jasper fancied he knew the face, but was not, in his haste, able to examine it closely. 'You were coming to me,' said Jasper, breathlessly, 'do me the favour to step in.'

'No ceremony friend,' said the stranger, in a hollow voice, 'walk on, show thy guests the way!'

There was no time to stand on ceremony. The wicket stood open, Jasper went up the staircase, the person following him. Jasper fancied that people were walking about his rooms. 'What devilry is this,' thought he, and hurried in – but here his legs gave way. The room was full of animated corpses. The moon shining through the windows, lit up their yellow and blue faces, sunken mouths, dull half-closed eyes, and thin protruding noses. Jasper recognised in them with dread people who had been buried with his aid; and, in the guest whom he had preceded, a Brigadier who had been interred in the cemetery, a couple of hundred yards off. All the women and men assembled surrounded the undertaker, bowing and greeting him; all except one poor fellow who carried his head under his arm. He was a pauper and had been buried by Jasper in that fashion through a mistake in the measurement. He seemed shy and ashamed of his tatters and did not venture to come forward, but stood retiredly in a corner. The rest were respectably dressed, the women wore caps with ribbons, those men who had served the State were in uniform, but their faces were unshaven; merchants wore their holiday clothes. 'See'st thou, Berryman,' said the Brigadier in the name of the company, 'how we have all risen at your invitation? Those alone have remained at home who could not possibly come, who had been unable to resist the influences which mother earth set to work upon their frail frames, but even thus, one of them could not rest – so anxious was he to see thee.'

At that moment a small skeleton pushed his way through the crowd and approached Jasper. His skull smiled affectionately at the undertaker, bits of light green and red cloth, and old linen, hung here and there about him, as upon a pole, whilst the bones of his feet rattled in his Hessian boots, like a pestle in a mortar.

'Thou dos'nt recognise me, Berryman' said the skeleton. 'Dosn't thou remember the retired sergeant, Peter Cox, of the Devon Fencibles, the same for whom thou soldest thy first coffin in the year '74 – and one of pine for one of oak?' So saying, the corpse extended his bony arms towards him; but Jasper, mastering all his strength, cried out, and pushed him from him. Peter Cox tottered, fell, and went to pieces.

A murmur of indignation was heard amongst the dead; they stood up for the honour of their companion, threatening and upbraiding Jasper; and the poor host, deafened by their cries, and almost pressed to death, losing his presence of mind, fell across the bones of the retired sergeant of the Fencibles and became unconscious. The sunlight had long been streaming across the bed on which the undertaker was sleeping. At last he opened his eyes, and saw before him the maid, blowing the fire. He was silent, expecting the girl to commence the conversation, and to relate to him the result of last night's adventures.

'How thee hast overslept thyself Jasper Berryman, sir,' said Ruth handing him his dressing gown. 'They neighbours, the tailor and the watchman, came asking thee to come out as it was Boxing Day, but thee was pleased to sleep and we did not like to wake'ee.'

'And did they come to me from the late Mrs Reddaway?'

'Late! Is her daid then?'

'Fool! that thou art! did'st not thou thyself help me to arrange things for her funeral.'

'Have'ee lost thee senses, sir? or ain't'ee got over last night's fuddle? What funeral was there yesterday? Thee did'st feast at the shoemaker's all day, and coming home tipsy, did'st throw thyself on thy bed, and has't slept until this very hour!'

'Indeed,' said the rejoiced undertaker.

'Of course,' answered Ruth.

'Well if that is the case, let me have some milk. And do you run down to the corner and get a quarter of rum. I am awful shaky and feel half dead; and I want a different sort of corpse-reviver to that I had last night.'

The Haunted Roadside Cottage

TJN

1881

'Once upon a time,' as they say in the fairy tales, an invalid lady in Exeter was recommended by her medical adviser to retire for a short season into the country for the benefit of her health. Naturally the question then arose as to the neighbourhood to which the good lady should repair for her temporary residence; and, after due consideration, it was decided that she should place herself for a while under the care of an old lady who occupied a cottage in a somewhat sequestered sot, not a hundred miles from the Halfway House on the Sidmouth Road.

Arriving at her destination, the visitor found the appearance of the old ivy-clad cottage, both internally and externally, to be dismal and weird; but its depressing influences were soon overcome to a great extent by those brought to bear on her by the very genial disposition of her hostess and the abounding interest of the neighbourhood. During the first day nothing was brought to the notice of the visitor to cause her the least alarm or fear; but early in the evening her hostess divulged a 'secret' which totally unnerved her for the rest of the night.

The story, with which she had horrified her newly arrived guest, was briefly this. Many years ago the cottage was occupied by an old hag, who, strange to say, had a very comely daughter. A swain in the village near fell deeply in love with the girl, and the affection being reciprocated, the happy couple began to think about joining themselves together in bonds which no man dare rend asunder. As often happens, when the news of their intended marriage became known to the girl's mother, a widow, the latter positively refused to give her consent to the union, for which conduct, however, she would advance no reason. Notwithstanding this, the ardent couple determined to marry, but so chagrined became that mother that she resolved to prevent the wedding by some means or other, fair or foul.

It happened that on one unlucky night the mother and daughter were engaged in a most desperate quarrel, and, sad to tell, the old woman struck the girl a blow which laid her lifeless on the floor of the bedroom in which the unhappy dispute took place. For a moment the wretched woman failed to realise the horrible result of her violence; but ensuing pangs of terror and remorse soon caused her to put an end to her own existence with the same instrument with which she had slain her daughter.

Early the following morning a visit of the girl's betrothed to the cottage brought the terrible tragedy to light, and crowds from the surrounding villages flocked to the scene.

For many years afterwards the cottage remained untenanted, no one daring to inhabit a dwelling which very speedily obtained the name of the 'haunted house'. The owner, having found this to be the case, determined to reside there himself, and did so, despite the warnings and entreaties of the superstitious villagers. For some time he lived among them, though not in very great comfort, having also been at last induced to believe that the dwelling was haunted by the spirits of the old woman and her child.

At his death he left the mysterious

piece of property to the narrator of the story, who had served him many years as his housekeeper. Having a moderate income, the old lady was enabled to live in the cottage without having to work for sustenance. But circumstances compelled her to use one downstairs room only, which sufficed for bedroom, parlour, kitchen and hall, the other chambers being locked up and used solely by a couple of ghosts, who very generously honoured the cottage with a visit every night, at that witching hour when, we are told, 'churchyards yawn' and uneasy spirits indulge in periodical promenades.

But the worst of the story was yet to be told. In the very chamber which had been assigned to the visitor, there was nightly to be witnessed a ghostly enactment of the dreadful tragedy before mentioned, whilst a sound could be distinctly heard as of some person vainly endeavouring, like Lady Macbeth, to wash indelible blood stains from his or her hands.

The narration of this and similar tale so engaged the attention of the couple that it was near midnight before the visitor proceeded to retire to rest. As might have been expected, the visitor was greatly agitated and extremely nervous as she mounted the creaking stairs en route to her bed chamber. Having reached the door to her room, she tremblingly pushed it ajar. As she did so she read a sound as of rippling water – a sound like unto that which would be caused by the washing of one's hands. With an effort she peered anxiously into the semi-darkness of the room, and straightway strange fancy conjured up a dreadful vision of murder and suicide. Overwhelmed with terror, her weak brain reeled. A moment later the room began to fill with smoke, and its atmosphere became insufferably warm. Was this too, a ghostly visitation?

No. The simple truth was that the frightened woman's candle had fallen from her hand, had ignited the furniture and set the room on fire. Luckily for the two half-crazy females, a 'revel' had been held in an adjacent village, and some of the folks who were passing, having heard the cries of the lady of the house and her visitor, and being assured that it was from human beings and not from some shrieking ghosts, that they proceeded, managed, with great difficulty, to rescue them from their position of peril.

Ineffectual efforts were made to stay the fire, and the next day and many days which followed that, the ruins were visited by an awe-filled rural crowd. The four charred walls of the cottage were all that the devouring flames suffered to remain; and on one of these being pulled down a solution to the blood-washing mystery was obtained.

Immediately behind where this wall had stood there was discovered a very small stream of water which issued from a spring on some elevated ground, and fell to the earth with a low gurgling sound, thick undergrowth concealing the spot. Thus it will be seen how, in the solemn quietness of the night, the ears of the nervous people caught the music of the rippling water, and fancy, fed by superstition, put its own interpretation on the mysterious sound. With regard to the strange visions, there remained no doubt in the minds of all reasonable persons that they proceeded from the same fertile source.

In this fashion was cleared up what was for many years a dreadful and insoluble mystery. But superstition lingers like a Metropolitan fog; and for a long

time after these occurrences the old folk of the surrounding villages were wont to point with awe the spot where once the dwelling stood, and shudder as they related the story of the
    HAUNTED ROADSIDE COTTAGE.

The Ghosts of Grimsby Grange

TJN

1880

'Somebody died!' ejaculated old Miss Quizington, her hand trembling as she looked at the black-bordered envelope put into her hand by the postman.

The worthy lady in question was housekeeper in general to the kind, whole-souled owner of Grimsby Grange, an old family mansion, situate in a somewhat dismal part of a high road, a mile or two from Exeter.

Mr Merryman, of Grimsby Grange, was, as Miss Q. would say, 'one of the olden times', being a firm believer in the strength of the ties growing out of mutual respect and appreciation which were wont to bind together master and servant; but which, unhappily, are fast disappearing in these 'enlightened days'. On the whole, Miss Q had, as she would often remark, 'a purty good time of it'.

'Somebody dead!' she again exclaimed, 'I thought this would be the end of it. I knew there was some back luck in store. There was the mice a-singing and running about the ceiling like fun last night; that cock would make up his mind to crow three times at midnight; and the death-watch too! Dearly me! I thought something was going to happen. The clock run down last night, and there was that great black spider a-stuck against the wall, and I couldn't move 'im, not even with a floor brush. Ugh! It makes me cream all over! And how unfortunate I should have upset that chair; and let the scissors fall and stick in the ground. Those four magpies, too, that I met in the road! Ah, me!' And with a shudder and a sigh, the superstitious old lady ran over the Devonshire ditty –

One, the sign of anger;
Two, the sign of mirth;
Three, the sign of marriage;
Four, the sign of death.

'What's this?' said she, as, after trembling opening the letter, she caught sight of the signature before there had been time to unfold it. 'From my niece, Mary. Her poor mother dead, I suppose. Always some bad luck in that family. Dear, dear; what a world to live in!'

'Come, come now. Taint so bad after all,' said the old lady in a more cheerful tone, and heaving a sigh of relief as she read:

Dear Aunt, I have made up my mind to come and see you, and you may expect me tomorrow morning. Excuse this mourning envelope as I have no other at hand.

Your affectionate niece, Mary

'There now,' exclaimed Miss Quizington, laying down the letter, and crossing her arms on her breast. 'To think of her frightening me like this – I must talk to her,' and Miss Q. endeavoured, though vainly, to put on an expression of gravity.

But, eccentric as she was, the old lady was exceedingly fond of her niece, and she toddled hither and thither making preparations for the pleasing visit. Getting this little delicacy and tidying that room, she moved briskly about until hot and exhausted, although it was at the coldest season of the year.

'As I breathe, here she comes,' said

Miss Q., peering out of the window across the meadow. 'And a young man with her! Well, I never!' And down to the door she made her way.

'How very tired you must be,' remarked the old lady kindly.

'Yes,' replied Mary. 'I should never have got here, but for this young gentleman,' pointing to Trudge, a young fellow who had the reputation of being in love with all pretty maidens in the village and who was now standing at the off side of the verandah with Mary's luggage.

'Oh! Mr Trudge, is that you?' asked Miss Quizington.

Mr Trudge was of opinion that it was himself, and smiled approvingly, as though to indicate that on the whole he thought he did himself credit.

'Come inside, both of you', said the now pleased old lady. 'Now sit down, Mary, and make yourself at home – don't wait to be asked what you want. I have put on the kettle, and you'll excuse me while I run and see what master wants.' And the dapper old lady went off, in answer to Mr Merryman's bell.

Mary was an affectionate niece, but she was very willing on this occasion to be left alone with Mr Trudge, for she, as many before her had done, had literally fallen in love with him. The couple had met (casually, of course!) in the meadow at the rear of Grimsby Grange, which Mary had to pass through on her road. Mary was in truth a 'pretty' girl, and Mr Trudge was not much to blame for allowing his feelings to obtain expression in all the eloquence which he could summon under the inspiration of the moment. They talked 'sweet nothings' for half an hour or more, but it seemed to the young folk that only a few moments had passed, when Aunt's footsteps were heard on the stairs, upon which Mr Trudge discreetly observed, in a louder tone than the rest of the conversation had been carried on in, that he thought he 'had better be going'.

'Don't go *already*, Mr Trudge,' said Aunt coaxingly. 'You will find Mary pleasant company.'

Trudge looked at Mary; she blushed modestly; and he remarked to himself that he was well aware of it. But in such a case, when one is most willing to stay, it is usual to remark that you have some important and pressing business to attend to, and Mr Trudge accordingly discovered that this presence was required in town that day.

'I am sorry to hear that,' said the vexed old lady. 'But let me give you a drop of cider before you go,' and without waiting for her offer to be accepted or rejected, off she went to the pantry with a huge mug. The cider was brought, and such cider as only Devonshire can produce. Trudge drank the nectar with an evident relish.

'I am sorry, sir, I did not hear you ring,' stammered Miss Quizington as she suddenly caught a glimpse of her master at the door.

'Neither did I ring,' remarked Mr Merryman, with a smile, 'I was not aware you had company –'.

'I feel vexed I did not acquaint you sir; but I didn't know anyone was coming, until I had a letter this morning. I am so sorry I have not asked your permission.'

'Oh! don't trouble,' said her good-hearted master. 'Had I known they were coming, we could have made better preparation for them, you know. It is unfortunate that business calls me out today. However, you'll provide your guests with every comfort, and I'll try to join you early in the evening,' and, with his customary pleasant smile, he quitted the room.

Conversation was now freely indulged, abundant praises of Mr Merryman being poured out. Ultimately the charms of Mary were eulogised, and Trudge, thinking the present harmonious time a fitting opportunity, ventured in her aunt's presence, to 'pop the question' to Mary. But little did he think that when he 'popped' the effervescence would be of such a nature as it proved.

'Mary, Mary! Did you ever hear tell of such imper'ence,' exclaimed Miss Q., who, instead of looking at the affair in a favourable light, had become incensed at the great breach of improprieties.

'Well,' replied the disappointed Trudge, 'Let Mary answer for herself.'

Mary was perplexed; and, not knowing what to say, very discreetly said nothing.

Trudge was evidently of the opinion

that 'silence gave consent' and, as he proceeded to quit the house, he smiled gratefully.

But Aunt Quizington's ruffled temper was not so easily smoothed. Taking Trudge by the shoulders, she hustled him out of the house with a briskness that astonished each one concerned. Making a false step, the agitated Trudge fell over the stone stairs, and as he arose he could not but remark *sotto voce* that Miss Q.'s biceps were in extremely good condition.

'Don't let me catch you here again,' said she shaking at him a plump hand, well decorated with flour and stray raisins, constituents of the Christmas which the dear old soul had just began to mix when the conversation took such an unexpected turn.

Mr Trudge notified his intention of considering the matter, and proceeded on his way.

'I am sorry,' said Mary some time afterwards, 'that you sent him away like that. He is a nice young fellow, and I confess I like him.' She feared to say 'love him' although that was what she meant.

'My dear child,' said her old aunt, patronisingly, 'you should not be so silly. Depend upon it, my dear, you make a very grand mistake – yes, a very grand mistake. I was never troubled by these bothering men.

In which remark there was much truth, for, somehow or other, those 'bothering men', young or old, handsome or otherwise, had never made up their minds to trouble him, for, though an excellent housekeeper and maiden aunt, she had not in her youthful days been gifted with any superabundance of personal charms and she had long been on the 'wrong side of thirty'.

However, she had no desire to cause

her niece any unhappiness, and, to divert the poor girl's thoughts from her absent swain, proposed to show her around the Grange, a treat Mary could by no means refuse.

It was a long ranging old building, one portion of which was occupied. One entire wing had the reputation of being haunted, and so fearful were the inhabitants of Grimsby Grange of the nocturnal visits, that every room (save one) had been closed for nearly half-a-century, and no one cared to be in the vicinity of the haunted chambers after dark. In the floor of the room that was occasionally entered (by day) was a large hole through which one could be seen the grim-looking walls of a disused cellar. Down here Aunt and Mary gazed until their imaginations conjured up phantoms which made their blood run cold, and, with a shudder, they quitted the haunted wing, and sought the brightness of the sitting room at the front of the house.

An agreeable tea over, Mary, whose curious appetite the visit to the haunted wing had whetted (for women are constitutionally curious) requested her aunt to tell her all she knew about the Ghosts of Grimsby Grange.

Nothing pleases old folk more than to be permitted to talk much and to be listened to attentively, and Aunt Q., being of this nature, yielded readily to her niece's request.

She then related how for many years the haunted chambers had never been entered. No one knew exactly why, but the reputation they enjoyed had come down from a remote period, and certain it was that strange sounds could be heard at night, which could be accounted for by no other theory than that of ghosts – at least, the people at Grimsby Grange rejected any other suggested solution of the problem as an insult to their common sense, and nobody had yet been bold enough to attempt to pacify their scepticism by penetrating the domains of the ghosts at this witching hour. Every night, then, said Aunt Quizington, the tenants of the haunted wing, were to be heard running about with light footsteps as though fleeing from some pursuer or indulging in ghostly gambols. Ever and anon they were heard to fall with a muffled thud, and their piteous moans and groans would follow. It was told that curious lights were occasionally to be observed flitting up and down and to and fro in the corridors and various chambers. Shrieks, groans, and fiendish laughter would follow, then a terrible gust of wind would extinguish all the phantom lights, and the ghostly performance for that occasion would terminate. The same programme, with or without the lights, would be gone through each night.

Scarce had Aunt Quizington finished her story than darkness set in – for December nights are early. Seeing, by the timorous glances she cast around the now weird-looking old room, and at the various old pieces of furniture it contained, that her niece was getting extremely nervous, Mrs Q. prepared the lights without asking Mary's assistance.

The chill which had fallen on the girl's spirits was removed for a time by the bright contrast of the lighted room with the vague twilight which had closed in around them while Aunt Quizington was telling the story of the Ghosts of Grimsby Grange. But as the evening wore on, the feeling returned. Nine o'clock arrived. Tired of conversing, they drew nearer to the hearthstone, and sought by stirring the fire to disperse the gloom that was assailing them. How very solemn seemed the silence of that old house. Even the measured ticking of the clock that stood in the corner added a peculiar terror of its own by making the silence even more palpable. Outside, a storm which had been threatening for some time had burst, and was momentarily gaining in force. The wind moaned and shrieked as it swept along the corridors and whistled ominously through the keyholes, often nearly extinguishing the flickering candle flame, as forcing open the door so suddenly as to make the good couple start with fright. It is not necessary to be superstitious to conceive the tension of such a situation.

Aunt Q. at length confessed to being a little nervous, for Mr Merryman had promised to return early. Going to the window she drew the curtain aside and gazed out into the night. The snow-storm increased rather than abated and she retired from the window shivering, but more from nerves than cold. Looking at the clock, she saw it was Eleven.

Her consternation at Mr Merryman's continued absence was very great. She had never dared to be out of her bedroom so late before. Even had she not been awaiting her master's return, she felt she could hardly venture on the journey thither, for the staircase, which led to the haunted chambers, would have to be passed, and the hour at which the Ghosts would begin their revels was near at hand. There was no alternative but to sit and wait.

Hush! What is that? A pattering of feet is heard up and down the stairs. Strange sounds proceed from the haunted chambers. 'The ghosts!' exclaim aunt and niece in a sort of suppressed scream, as they draw nearer to each other.

Hark again! A heavy footstep is heard, and, with a patter, a hasty retreat from the object is evidently made. Horror! The footsteps have passed out from the haunted chamber, and are evidently proceeding from the common staircase. Yes, you may hear the heavy step, and as it deliberately comes down the stairs, the hearts of the poor women seem to sink with them. It has reached the bottom, but it does not stay there. Rushing forward it strikes the door a blow. The affrighted couple jump out of their seats and look fearfully at the door.

'Whatever shall we do?' gasps Aunt.

'It demands admission, it will be the worse for us if we deny it.' She might just as well have asked the poor cockroach she had just crushed, as Mary. For a moment they were again silent, but the silence only served to make the gloom more terrible.

'Why should we fear?' Mrs Q ventures at length to enquire. 'I never harmed anybody, and if it is a ghost, may God help me.'

Taking a candle in her hand, she bids Mary follow her, and approaches the door. At length she ventures to open it! And what follows? The 'fiend' has not fled, but, as if aware of the couple's intentions, is waiting in preparedness outside.

The 'ghost' strikes the trembling old woman a blow that staggers her, and a wild gust of wind extinguishes the light. They are now in darkness in the presence of ghosts! And, faint with fear, they shriek and sink to the ground.

Two forms stand over and seize them. Heavens! Who are they? Two solid for ghosts? Then they must be housebreakers! No! They speak too kindly for that.

The poor creatures revive and what do they find? Mary, that she is in the arms of Trudge, and Aunt, that she is being supported by her master, both of whom had been attracted to the spot by their shrieks.

On what followed that night I will not dwell.

Next morning, amid mingled vexation and mirth everything was explained. A thorough search in the haunted dwelling was made by Mr Merryman and Trudge. The ghosts were soon 'laid'. The mysterious footsteps turned out to be the noise occasioned by the running about of a large number of rats; and the heavy thuds which had been so unaccountable were the sounds made by the large wooden ball being rolled by the playful quadrupeds about the floor of the 'haunted chamber'. The shrieks and groans were occasioned by the wind; and, as for the ponderous steps of the ghost who came downstairs, it was plainly shown that the rats that night in trundling about the ball had forced it out of the room and over the stairs, when it, of course, forcibly struck against the door.

Everything being thus explained, Trudge ventured to enquire what had occurred to frighten the ladies. Much to the merriment of Trudge and the Grimsby owner, Aunt and Mary confessed to fainting, the former because she thought she saw a ghost and the latter because she saw – a rat.

The remainder of the day was happily spent. Mr Merryman remarked that, after the manner in which Trudge had served to clear up the mysteries of the Grange, he deserved some consideration. He and Mary seemed fond of each other, and he was of opinion that the match would be a good one to which Aunt could not now offer objection.

The approbation of all concerned

being obtained, one day, not long afterwards, an admiring gathering of villagers beheld a couple wend their way up the aisle of the little church; and heard a good old clergyman proclaim them man and wife.

Time passes on. Sitting, in the cool of a summer evening, in a pretty little rustic porch, Mary and her husband hear the village church bells ringing gaily. As they listen thoughts, happy thoughts, of their wedding day possess they think of the bliss they have experienced, and how it was brought about by

THE GHOSTS OF GRIMSBY GRANGE.

GHOST STORY

TICKLER
1864

In order, first, to launch by rhyme,
Know, friends, that 'once upon a time'
A ghost appear'd in Kenton town,
Which lieth south, some sev'n miles down
From Exon, where one Tuckett dwelt,
Who could e'en ghosts to nothing melt;
And at whose wink, or nod, or cough,
Sir Lucifer would 'missle' off;
Or, perhaps, the plainer words to put,
The very devil himself would cut.

But, first of all to clear the case,
Let me in brief describe the place:
The main part is a straggling street

(no matter as to yards or feet),
And half of which, it will be found,
Compriseth parish burial ground,
Where, villagers can swear by hosts,
They've heard and witness'd 'rayal' ghosts.
I've heard old grandf'er Bickford say
That once upon his homeward way,
Just at the solemn midnight hour,
He heard a voice say, from the tow'r,
'Now Gran'fer make haste hom; d'ee yer?
Thee hast no right away vrim HER';
And when he got home heard the 'larm',
That his 'old dumman'd brauk her arm'.
And one time, earlier e'en than that,
He saw a large two-headed cat,
Upon a tombstone stood upright,
And holding out his paws so tight,
As grandf'er stood there, like a stone,
He heard two voices say 'com on!'
He'd been a 'good man' in his day,
But 'vight way gosts' said he, 'laur jay!'
He didn't care to have a 'scat',

'Wen thare wiz nort a tal ta hat'.
Well, then, I'e heard old Cherry Eyres,
Who trades in small grocery wares,
Declare that, one night, going to bed,
Opposite to where rest the dead,
She really thought she must have died,
To see, just where her old man lied,
A light all blue and white ascend,
As if its height would never end;
And just as she began her pray'rs;
Her Jan's voice sung out 'Cherry Eyres!
Luke in tha geard'n, gie dree knocks,
An, wen yu yer ma cal, a box
Will, herry deer, ta aize ma zaul,
Spring tu thy voot up droo a haul:
Thares veefty poun' that I'd a save,
Bevaur I went to me zilent grave;
I shud a told'ee at that nick –
A-time, bit as tuk'd off too quick'
Just then she heard a 'clap of thunder',
And, in her fright, 'shet tu tha winder',
The light went out, she went to bed,

VICTORIAN GHOST STORIES

And heard no more of the old man dead.
I asked her how about the knocks,
And whether she found the money box;
She told me with a sorrowful face,
She'd giv'n three knocks, but 'twad'n tha place';
In fact, she had knock't the 'geard'n' over,
But couldn't the hidd'n gold discover;
Yet, strong in faith, to the day she died,
She would'nt believe 'es ghost had lied';
She miss'd the spot that 'exack he named'
But it 'wad'n hee thit was ta be blamed,
Vur that vorty yer that her wiz ez wife
Ha'd niver a tole her a lie in ez life,
An za sure ez hur old cat wid purdle,
Ha wid'n du et in tother wurdle.'
But 'I'll knock and knock' the old soul said,
'For at least it may tell the old man dead,
Tho'et dith no aithly gude-ta me,
I honour'd the last wurds zed be hee'.
But I'm running on in measure wild,
And my gentle muse saith – draw it mild,
Methinks you will have got to glory,

Before you reach your promised story,
Dear muse allow me just to say,
You meeting trouble are half way,
I've only giv'n a case or two,
To show what ghosts and goblins do;
But as you're in a hurried way,
I'll tell the tale of Fanny Bray,
Promising (for its much the same)
'Tis only an adopted name.
Old Fanny was a quiet soul,
Who burnt up wood instead of coal –
Because the one was got for 'nort'
The other, as she said, was 'bort'
So of the two she'd rather fix
Upon the course of picking sticks.
Time was when gentlefolk would give
The poor around a chance to live
Thro' winter, free from legal harm,
For picking sticks to keep them warm,
Until the county 'bobbies' came,
And made the sticks as scarce as game,
'Hood picking' in the good old time,

Was honesty, but now 'tis crime,
Brought in by 'sich' as Lady Rolle –
'The Laurd ha massy pin her soul',
I heard a poor 'hoodpicker' say,
Who'd to the prison found his way,
Because he had taken to himself
Some twopence worth of wooden pelf.
No doubt such a law will come in soon
To send such culprits to the moon;
Where one poor chap, for years untold,
Hath in that dismal planet rolled
For having, when 'twas cold and windy,
Pick'd up a stick or two on 'Zindy'.
All I can say's – I'd have a clause
If such e'er be among our laws:
To make each prosecutor pace
Straight to the moon, to prove his case;
And in such trivial offences
Just make him pay his own expenses.
But I'm digressing, you will say,
'And what about old Fanny Bray?'
Well, Fanny wasn't to be done,

And had for many years been one,
To ramble where she cared or could,
Her object being 'picking hood'.
The Bobbies knew her, but 'No go'.
She'd smell 'em for a mile or so.
And thus for years her sticks she scrap'd,
And from their tender mercies 'scaped.
Twas said her escapades were 'sich'
That Fanny Bray must be a witch;
And, being such a weird old crony,
Must be, of course, possess'd of money,
But there's a 'Bobby' who, one day,
Laid his strong hand on Fanny Bray.
This 'Bobby' wasn't dress'd in blue,
With buttons running all down through;
He had no cudgel in his hand
With which to make offenders 'stand';
His face was measured, firm yet slow,
His lightest touch a knock-down blow;
Paralysis was in his breath,
This Bobby's name, my friends, was 'Death'.
In silence he'd around her gone,

She never heard him say 'move on'.
And thus it is, from day to day,
We live on in a careless way;
By our own heedlessness defended,
Until at last we're apprehended:
Twas for this self-same heedless way
The Peeler Death took Fanny Bray;
For this she got into a fix,
But not for picking a few sticks.
What was it then's the question giv'n
That kept poor Fan from going to Heaven;
For she was seen, or else folk lied,
In her old house the night she died;
And at her window, every night,
For weeks appear'd in lurid light,
At twelve o'clock, as 'safe's a gun',
And sometimes quite so late as one,
She at her window would appear,
As if just risen from her bier;
And there she'd stay some half the night,
Envelop'd with most awful light,
Till all at once she'd flash away,

Perhaps she feared the approach of day.
One night, just after she was gone,
Jan Morrish, with his night-cap on,
Look'd in the room, and 'smul'd a smul'
And for weeks after 'wad'n wul'
And, when he came out from the dark,
Upon his night-cap was a mark.
'Yu niver', said he, 'zeed tha feller
Awt; twas Brimstone cuz 'twizz yeller'.
Well, soon the news got spread abroad,
And every night the middle road
Was thronged by such an eager host
Of folks to see the Kenton Ghost.
A local preacher had 'a pray'
To drive poor Fanny's ghost away;
But not a bit of use was that –
In spite of all there still she sat.
'Twas said, 'Hur wid'n laive her perch,
Cuz Pass'n C. warn't in the church'.
One day the daughter of poor Fan
To Exon came to see the man,
Who, of all others, knew the way,

'Twas said a 'thousand ghosts to lay'.
The learned man was surnam'd Tuckett,
And once had found Fan's 'darter's' bucket.
He gave her sev'ral little stones,
Tied in a bab, and said Fan's bones
Would knock against her coffin lid,
That's 'if so be' her 'darter' did
Say 'picksy, wicksy, rum, tum, tee'.
Twice for each stone – no harm in three.
The spirit then would hear the bones,
And after giving several groans,
Her form would then like smoke be curl'd,
And straight be off for tother world.
She paid the wise man, home she came,
And tired that night her 'little game';
And as she finished 'rum um, tee',
A lot of folks as well as she
Heard old Fan's voice cry out aloud,
And saw her form roll like a cloud
Away; and never since that night
Have people seen that fearful sight.
Some said the moon, with curious light,

Was on the window 'shining bright'
And there were other folks that vow'd
'Twas nothing but a passing cloud
That, with a slow and solemn pace,
Was floating 'neath her moonship's face;
And in this manner, moving pass,
Threw its dark shadow on the glass.
And that the rain came on that night,
And from that time the curious light
From that sole cause had ceased to be,
And not from 'wicksy, rum, tum, tee'.

A Devonshire Ghost Story

G. SEAGE
1896

It was a Christmas of the old fashioned sort. The snow lay thick, crisp, and white upon the ground while the red berries gleamed out in bright profusion from their fantastic setting of rich green leaves – leaves which contrasted strongly with the dainty delicately tinted mistletoe which hung over the doorway of the quaint, but not very commodious, school room which constituted the most important building in a small Devonshire town. It was a picturesque portion of the county, which has now been touched by the railway line, but which, at the time of my story, stood, as it were, within a little world of its own, jealously cherishing its time-honoured traditions and cleaning to its old-world customs. The little world thus indicated was agitated by a flutter of exhilaration more than usually pronounced even at that joyous season by the fact that to the Christmas festivities were added those attendant upon the coming of age of good old Squire Western's eldest son, the heir to Thornley.

There had been a mighty consumption of roast beef and plum pudding and a prodigious quantity of 'Old October' brewed specially for the auspicious event, and which had a reputation of having attained an age equivalent to that at which the prospective squire had arrived, and disappeared. Toast and singing had flown merrily round, and a jolly looking young fellow, with a fresh healthy complexion and a frank open countenance was relating, more or less musically, the adventures of certain persons who borrowed an old mare from an obliging friend whom they familiarly styled 'Tom Pearse' and who, consistent with tradition, lost both his beast and his friends as the result of his trustfulness.

The poet thus describes the sad sequel to the generosity of friend Tom:

When the wind whistles cold on the moor of a night,
All along, down along, out along loe,
Tom Pearse's old mare doth appear, ghostly white,
Wi' Bill Brewer, Jan Stewer, Peter Gurney,
Peter Davy, Dan Whiddon,
Harry Hawk and Uncle Tom Cobleigh and all.

And all the long night he heard skirting and groans,
From Tom Pearse's old mare in her rattling bones,
And from Bill Brewer &c

The singing of the old Devonshire ditty, which enabled its bearers to indulge in long chorus, repeated after each two or three lines of narrative verse, was followed by hearty applause and some laughter, upon which a venerable old villager – the real, live, oldest inhabitant of the neighbourhood – chimed in with a story about certain rustic and highly respectable ghosts who had come within the scope of his experience, including that of a deceased tom cat who had been a venerable retainer in his father's house, and whose spirit form was always to be seen and its voices heard in woeful caterwaulings when death was about to visit the household.

A stalwart young policeman was standing near the door, ostensibly for the purpose of seeing that everything was carried out 'with decency and in order' but who evidently seemed more anxious to take into custody the smart little waitress from the 'Cat and Fiddle' who was whisking about with the good things in requisition. But he had a rival in young Bob Stemson, the lad who just been singing, and both were intent upon winning the smile of the comely daughter of the local carrier – Long Luke, as he was called, from the extreme longitude of his proportions. Mr Luke was not what might be generally regarded as an ideal father-in-law. He drank huge quantities of ale, smoked like a volcano in eruptions and was of an erratic and disagreeable temper. Still, the charms of the daughter more than outweighed, in the opinion of her admirers, the defects of the father. On the occasion in question Long Luke had partaken plenteously of the good cheer provided and after waxing argumentative for a time had subsided into a state of peaceful somnolence, from which he was not aroused until nearly all the company had dispersed.

At twelve o'clock that night Constable Davey was perambulating his lonely beat. A portion of the ground which he had to cover led through the Churchyard, and as he drew near to this portion of his peregrinations thoughts arose within him of the ghost stories which the old folks had related at that day's merry-making. His previous meditations had been of the trim little lass from whom he had snatched a kiss, under the mistletoe, when 'no one was looking' unconscious of the fact that young Stemson had preceded him by only a few moments in a similar clandestine operation. To turn from dreams so bright to ghostly considerations was not pleasant, but feelings will sometimes come over one in a churchyard, at the dead of night, which would not trouble one in the brightness and beauty of day.

The 'midnight bell' had 'with its iron tongue and brazen mouth' sounded twelve 'unto the dreary race of night' and the last note was just dying away when the ear of the constable was arrested by a sound which seemed to proceed from below the surface of the ground not far from where he stood. It was as though some unquiet spirit was seeking to break through the confines of the grave. Petrified with superstitious dread, the constable gazed in the direction of the sound.

The soft rays of the moon were filtered on to a grassy mound through weird-looking trees which dropped over it, and by its light the constable saw at first a long, bony, claw-like hand protruding from the ground, then another, and then – oh, horrors of horrors – a livid, death-like head, in which were set deep, sinister, piercing eyes, which seemed to glare fiercely at the terrified onlooker. At first, the constable stood as one rooted to the spot, paralysed with fear and deprived of the power of motion. Then, with a fearful yell, he rushed madly from the spot.

Morning had dawned, and the pleasant haunts of the elves and pixies of Devonshire's fairyland – those mischievous imps which are said to have led so many good and true yeoman stray when returning from market to their hearths, their homes and their good dames – were basking in the kindly glances of honest old Sol, who was doing his best to wage successful battle with that terribly mischievous fellow, Jack Frost. A choice company were quaffing their ale and smoking their 'churchwardens' in the snug little parlour of the 'Cat and Fiddle'.

The topic of conversation was the adventure of Constable Davey, who, it was said, had seen a ghost in the churchyard, and who was now laid up on account of the shock to his nervous system. The story was being narrated for the fortieth time, when a new comer arrived in the form of Long Luke.

'Well,' said he, 'I've heard tell uv sum curyis things in me time, but thicky thare yarn o' yourn bayts cock-vighting.'

'Cock-vighting or hoss-racing; tis true, that's sartin. There's the Bobby haum to es lodgins, purty nigh vrightened tu death.'

'Ah,' said Luke, with more than usual satisfaction in his tone, 'I'll zune lay tha ghost and cure the Bobby tu, Whey, thic ghost was me.'

'You?' chorused the astonished audience.

'Ees, zure.' And then he told a story – which was, in effect, that coming through the churchyard on his way home from the festivities of the previous day he fell into an open grave, and remained unconscious for some time. Awakening, and finding his quarters far from comfortable, he hastened to get out. This he was in a fair way of doing, by inserting his toes into the mould on either side and thus raising himself to the surface, when just as he got his head above ground he was nearly frightened out of his wits by hearing an unearthly yell and seeing a huge black figure bounding across the ground.

'And that', added he, in conclusion, 'wuz tha p'leeceman. Wull, I'm danged! I shull marry my darter to Bob Stemson. Et zhant be zed that old Luke givved away his gal to a veller that runned auf an left es pore old vather-en-law in tha grave.'

And he kept his word.

The Devil and the Money-Hunters at Afton Castle

TICKLER

1865

Afton Castle is a mile or two from here, or rather the remains thereof, for the castle has been dismantled these many years. It is said that, in the time of the Protectorate – when Cromwell's army visited the West, and was nearly everywhere victorious, as it deserved to be – the family then living at the Castle, begin on the side of the Stuarts, and being likewise apprehensive that a 'clear sweep' would be made of all their valuables, gathered together the money they possessed, and, putting it into a huge iron crock, or 'chittle', buried it near the Castle.

To indicate the spot where the treasure was buried, fir trees were planted; and it was rumoured among the inhabitants of the neighbourhood that the spirits of former unsuccessful diggers were in the habit of 'troubling' the plantation. It was even said that the Evil One himself (together with his cloven hoof and tail) had been seen dodging behind the trees, as though guarding the treasure that was said to be concealed beneath it. Be that as it may, it was certain that old Jan Bustard, his wife Ruth and their two sons, Will and Jan, saw something that frightened them not a little, and to this day their progeny swear that it was the Devil that they saw.

But let me narrate the story as I have heard my grandmother tell it. On one fine Christmas Eve, then, Jan Bustard, his wife, and two sons, left their cottage with shovels, pickaxes, and ropes, determined to search, and if possible to find, the 'crock of gold' which was believed to be hidden in the bowels of the earth in the Castle plantation. It was, as I have said, a fine night; the stars shone bright, and so likewise did the moon.

Jan Bustard was a thick-set, grizzly-headed, bandy-legged old fellow – strong as a lion, and afraid of nothing. In his wife he had a good mate. Will was like his parents, but young Jan was a little timid-like, and didn't seem to relish going out of a Christmas Eve to dig in a plantation where spirits had been seen. He was, however, compelled to obey his parents' commands; but, truth to tell, young Jan followed with pick-axe on shoulder most unwillingly, and with 'fear and trembling'. Being the youngest of the party, he lagged behind, and, just as he was passing an old tumble-down house, where there is a large tree growing, young Jan heard the screech of an owl, and, then, as he thought, appeared a tall, giant, ghastly spectre. Like Bloomfield's Giles, under similar circumstances, Jan stopped,

And not a breath
Heaved from his heart, that sunk almost to death.
Loud the owl hallooed o'er his head unseen;
All else was silent, dismally serene.

'Feyther, feyther, tha ghost, tha ghost' ejaculated the shivering lad. 'Feyther' hearing a cry of distress, rushed back and found his son standing in the attitude of terror and dismay. 'Luke, luke, feyther', exclaimed Jan, as the same time pointing to the ghost –

A grisly spectre, clothed in silver grey
Around whose feet the waving shadows play,
Stood in his path!

Jan Bustard, the elder, looked in the direction of the spectre for a second, and only for a second, when, turning his grey eyes upon his boy and regarding him with supreme contempt, he ejaculated 'Why, thee vool, tis the old ash tree, where theest picked up the locks and keys many a Zummer time!'

Young Jan, being slowly convinced that his father was right, and that he had seen no ghost, but an old tree, and nothing but a tree, followed his father a little more cheerfully than he had previously done. On arriving at the plantation, all hands set to work at the spot where 'old Nick' (as Jan Bustard irreverently called the Evil One) had been seen the oftenest.

They dug down several feet, through the flinty, frosty soil, but nothing could they find. It was drawing near to midnight, and young Jan, being aware of that alarming fact, began to shiver and shake.

'Bear up Jan,' cried the father.

'Dig away, Will,' cried the mother.

'Hark! I'm blest if there isn't a clink!' exclaimed Will.

Immediately the clock struck twelve, and at that moment the diggers came upon a large iron pot.

'I'm beggared if here isn't the chittle' exclaimed Jan with glee.

'Lower the rope mauther,' he continued, and Ruth threw down the rope to her ecstatic husband. 'Pully hally, boys,' cried Jan, and pully-hally they did. Finally the 'chittle' was hauled to the surface, and Jan rubbed his hands with glee.

'In the name of God and the Devil we have got en!' exclaimed Ruth. At that moment a flame of fire flashed in the eyes of all of them; the clanking sound of chains was heard; and a tall man in black, with a tail – Ruth swore she saw that distinctly, for it wagged, as she believed in anger – suddenly stood before them.

Even brave old Jan's courage now forsook him; the vigour of young Jan's knees departed, for he fell groaning to the ground, whilst Ruth and Will knelt before 'Mr Devil' (as they designated him) and 'begged for forgiveness'.

The man in black in a voice that made the whole digging party quake, exclaimed, 'So long as Afton is Afton, never more shall the chittle be brought to the brim' upon which the crock fell into the pit, which appeared to fill up miraculously, for no hands were visible, and it was done in less time than I have taken to mention it. When this was done, Satan departed in a flash of lightning, and Jan Bustard, when he had a little recovered himself, called to his wife and said 'Come along soce – let's go hoam – and if I wance git thar I'm darned if I ivver hunts arter a chittle of money again on Christmas Eve!'

The Christmas in Devon Series

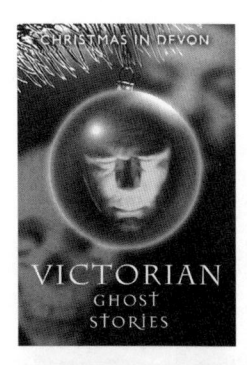

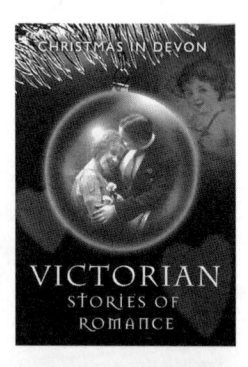

Also available from **The Mint Press**

Christmas in Devon (2001)
Victorian Stories of Exeter
Victorian Stories of Romance
Victorian Stories 'Round a Dartmoor Hearth

Christmas in Devon   Todd Gray (2000)

The Devon Almanac   Todd Gray (2000)

The Concise Histories of Devon Series
Roman Devon   Malcolm Todd (2001)
The Vikings and Devon   Derek Gore (2001)
Elizabethan Devon   Todd Gray (2001)
Devon and the Civil War   Mark Stoyle (2001)

The Devon Engraved Series
Exeter Engraved: The Secular City (2000)
Exeter Engraved: The Cathedral, Churches, Chapels and Priories (2001)
Devon Country Houses and Gardens Engraved (2001)
Dartmoor Engraved (2001)

The Travellers' Tales Series
Exeter (2000)
East Devon (2000)
Cornwall (2000)